Miss Lilly

Miss Lilly
My Life as a Feline Royal

Rikke Goldhirsh, Psy.D.

Wisdom Moon Publishing
2015

MISS LILLY: MY LIFE AS A FELINE ROYAL

Published by Wisdom Moon Publishing LLC

Wisdom Moon™, the Wisdom Moon logo™, *Wisdom Moon Publishing*™, and *WMP*™ are trademarks of Wisdom Moon Publishing LLC.

www.WisdomMoonPublishing.com

ISBN 978-1-938459-60-3 (softcover, alk. paper)
ISBN 978-1-938459-62-7 (eBook)

LCCN 2015951726

Cover images digitally modified from paintings by Ida Goldhirsh.

TABLE OF CONTENTS

Chapter One
Training My Human

This is my story; it is about me, Lailah, alias Miss Lilly. Even when I digress, it's still about me—my thoughts, my memories, and my understanding of life.

When I was 18 years old and still absolutely gorgeous, I lived in a log house with my two people, who I named My Human and Human Number Two; I call them My H and Two for short. We had other members of feline royalty living with us, their names as given to them by My H were: Shaba, Dreamy Coco, Ushuti Two Shoes, Sunkist (alias Miss Meepy), Kali Alley Kat Kay, and Charlie Sue Magoo. Outside there were two smelly beasts that kept the wild animals at bay with their noisy barking and, when need be, their growling. They were named Liquorish and Pete. Lest I forget and do not give you the full picture of the family, let me tell you that there were two huge, no enormous, gigantic "cans of dog food," as I called them, that lived in the barn and corral. The humans said one of them was a Fox Trotter Stallion and the other an Arabian Mare. The humans were foolish enough to pay good money for them and then pay to bring them to our property.

Worse yet, when My H was walking the Arabian Mare from the main road down to our driveway, she and the horse tripped over each other. My H fell face down on the dirt road and the mare rolled over her spine-to-spine. The horse was not hurt and My H sat up, a bit dazed but able to stand and walk. What possesses people to do such things? I think that My H had her Guardian Angel and untold other angels looking after her that day! She could have been crushed or paralyzed. Thanks for angels.

My H said later that the weight of the horse was unspeakably heavy and she herself was surprised she could get up on her own. The lady delivering the horse walked her the rest of the way past the log house into the corral.

The log house was small, but just right for living in the country. My H acted as her own contractor when building that log house and she and Two did much of the work themselves. It was very interesting watching them build the forms for the perimeter foundation and having the concrete poured. Then they set in the floor joists and nailed down the sub flooring. After the logs were raised, they put in the chinking and coated the logs with preservative. Later My H put in the tile floor and Two built a deck. We had a beautiful light-blue and white soapstone, wood-burning stove for the center of the downstairs living area. That came in really handy in the winter.

Speaking of winter, I was born on the coast and was not prepared for twenty-two degrees below zero with three feet of snow on the ground for days and weeks at a time. When I complained to My H for bringing me to such misery, she said we all had to follow our calling and go where the Spirit leads. That is good and fine for her, but what about me? I think she should have made her life conform to my needs and wants. In a way humans bully us felines by bossing us around. They think that because they have thumbs and we don't they are in control. They have a lot to learn.

I digress. More about me. My life started out very traumatically. When my mom was pregnant with me and my siblings and had the freedom of the streets, one day she was suddenly captured by heathens and thrown into a cell in what they called an animal shelter. That is where my siblings and I were born. As soon as we could be weaned, they wrenched us away from mom and put us in a big cage with about twenty other kittens. I never saw my mom again.

This type of treatment can really scar a kitten, but I am a survivor and I never let my trauma stop me from living a full life or accomplishing my life mission. You may wonder what mission a feline could have in life as we are assumed to be lesser than humans, so let me fill you in. My life experiences are shared with the soul group that I am an expression of. We all pool our learning, understandings, and experiences thereby enhancing each other and helping our whole group to advance. I think it is essentially the same for humans, as they have something like soul families.

Training my Human

Back to the cage at the shelter. I was way too young and way too small to be taken from my mom and subjected to those crowded, noisy conditions. Repeatedly, I told the caretakers that I did not belong there in that cage and deserved to be treated like the royalty that I am. No one listened. Finally, I started a habit of climbing the side of the wire cage and declaring my royalty. I would open my mouth as wide as I could, show all of my tiny little teeth and yell, "Meow, meow, meow!" When I did, I was so emphatic that my eyes crossed. The caretakers just went on about their business. Later in life I realized that I was probably lucky to be indoors with enough food and water and safety. At the time, I was not grateful.

When I was just about exhausted and despairing of ever being recognized for the grand being that I am, in walks a human female (the one that I later named "My Human"). When she first walked in I was busy climbing and exclaiming so I didn't pay much attention to her. She was smiling and said to her companion (later I found out this was Grandma), "Oh look at this cute little girl climbing up the side of the cage. She's gorgeous with black and grey tiger-stripe fur. Her little tummy hair is grey, but it almost looks green. Grandma said, "I think she needs a bath." My human said, "There are way too many kittens in that one cage. I have to rescue her."

When I first noticed them looking at me and smiling, I yelled at them as loud as I could. "Get me out of here! Take me with you!" They really had me going and I was hoping against hope for rescue until I heard the word, "bath." What an insult! We royals bathe ourselves, thank you very much! That is what I yelled at her as loud as I could, which was not very loud seeing as I was still so small and so tired from all the climbing and exclaiming.

Nonetheless, she did rescue me and did take me home. Unfortunately, she did have the insanity to bathe me. My Human did not get away with that bit of tyranny unscathed! I bit her and scratched her the whole time she was forcing me to undergo that humiliation. In the end she dried me and gave me some delicious kibble soaked in milk; there were bits of shrimp in it, too. I forgave her. I felt a little bad for having drawn blood on her arms with my claws, but you just have to teach these humans how to behave. Thankfully, she learned that lesson after just one training session. She has never bathed me again. I do it myself! Thank you very much!

In the beginning of our feline/human relationship we lived in a condo in the city. It was just me, My Human and Shaba, who had been rescued from a shelter before me. We lived in a fairly upscale neighborhood even though it was rather bohemian. It was never dull, what with dogs running loose in the neighborhood and other lesser-level royalty out wandering around getting into who knows what. I tell you, those, who wander around at all times of day or night sure have a different set of morals. I would never behave like that! Although, I suspect Shaba would have done it on the sly if he had had the chance! Not to worry... I had him under control. Male royalty are about as hard to keep tamed as humans are.

After much hard work, Shaba and I finally had My H well trained to serve our needs. In the city, she took us outside twice a day to sniff around and get all the neighborhood news. We had sunning time, sniffing time, rubbing opportunities, and our human to stand guard and keep us safe from the horde. One day when we were out exploring our territory and smelling the trails of those who had been hanging around in our absence, Shaba suddenly wheeled around and began howling at the top of his lungs. I had never heard such earthy tones from him! Then I saw it. A giant of a dog with humongous teeth and smelly, long fur all over his body. It was a big male German Shepherd. It had deigned to enter our territory! I was quaking from my paws, fearful of being eaten alive or left torn asunder.

"The audacity!" Shaba said as he took off after that mutt, jumped on his back while simultaneously sinking his teeth and claws into the nape of its giant's neck. That canine giant had tried to run when he saw Shaba coming so Shaba got him from the side. Let me tell you, that dog yelped and ran for the hills with Shaba still holding on and bouncing up and down on that mutt's side. Finally, Shaba let go, turned to make sure he did not have to go after the mutt again and then came strutting back to my side. That poor dog went yelping home on the run. He was never so foolish as to return to our territory ever again. Oh, did I tell you Shaba was twenty pounds of solid muscle. What a handsome guy; orange tabby he was! He made a great companion for me. After that day, I never doubted him again. I always felt safe with him around.

Okay, I have to tell you this: one time the three of us went for a drive in the early evening—me, My Human, and Shaba. It was dark out, but we had Shaba in the car so we weren't worried. (Note: when driving down the road, only My Human could be seen.) The car windows were open just a couple of inches and the vent windows in the front were open. When we were stopped for a light, a guy came walking up to the car on the passenger side and put his face in the vent window. Shaba jumped up from the floor hissing and the guy jumped up and back, shrieked, and went running off. That was awfully funny! Nothing to worry about with Shaba around!

Chapter Two
Expansion

While living in the condo, our family expanded. There was a feral clan of cats living under the house next door. This was an amazing group of felines as they had a whole community; they were cooperative with each other and looked out for each other. They had both verbal and non-verbal communication with each other, even from a distance. They had a language all their own. We other felines could understand some of their words, but not all of them. They could understand all of what we said, but their language was much more extensive and involved.

All of the males looked exactly alike and were very odd looking because they had very large elongated heads. Their fur was an off-white/light-grey color. The females were very sleek and gorgeous and all looked almost exactly alike. Nearly all of them had white as their base color with black markings. There was one of the young females who had the same pattern of markings but where everyone else had black, she had tan. We put food and water out for the clan as My H did not think they could find enough food and water on their own.

One of the mama feral cats kept bringing her two young kittens to play under the stairs in front of our living room window. We all spent time watching and enjoying their antics. Finally the mom and one kitten stopped coming around, but the other kitten kept coming over to play. This kitten had the beautiful black markings on her white fur just like her mom, only, she was even prettier. When the kitten had been coming around on her own without her mom for a while, My H said she had the intuition that the kitten needed to become part of the family.

One afternoon, when the kitten was about five or six months old, My H asked Shaba and me to stay inside while she went out with one of our toys. She left the front door open as she played and played with the kitten, using the toy. When she was finally able to lure the kitten close to the front door, she threw the toy inside. The kitten went running into the living area after the toy. It was then that My H rushed inside and suddenly closed the door behind her.

The kitten went wild. She was so frightened. She had never been closed-in before. She literally bounced off one wall about two feet above the ground, went running to the opposite wall, bounced off of it about two feet off the ground, back and forth, back and forth, bouncing off the walls. We all thought she was going to injure herself. My H was thinking she had made a mistake bringing the kitten inside when Shaba had enough. He walked over and placed himself in her path. The next time she came running by, he popped her on the head three times with the pads of his left paw. That kitten stopped in her tracks, looked at him, sat there a while and began to look around. That was it; she was part of the family and was never afraid of us or the indoors again.

We named her Ushuti Two Shoes. My H thought the name Ushuti was from a Sanskrit word that meant "curiosity" (signifying her curiosity about the toy that brought her into the condo) and the Two Shoes part got into the mix because she had two white shoes on her front paws, and black fur all the rest of the way up.

Two Shoes' mom came to visit her a couple of times to see how she was doing and then never came back again. We think she brought Two Shoes to us so she could have a good life with a human to care for her.

Oh, you ask, How did I get my name? Well, since I have black and grey tiger-stripe fur, I am named Lailah, which means "night" in Hebrew. Miss Lilly is one of my nicknames. Shaba? He was so young and so tiny when he came to live with My Human that she and the veterinarian thought he was a girl. My Human is one of the humans that recognizes our royal nature, so she gave him the name, Queen Sheba. Well, by the time it became obvious that he was a boy, he had already learned his name. So, My H thought it best to keep the "Sh" sound at the beginning and the "a" sound at the end. She knew "Shavasana" in Sanskrit signified the corpse pose and even though Shaba was anything but a relaxed kind of guy, she changed Sheba into Shaba. It worked out well; that cute little orange-and-white striped bundle of love and spitfire never even realized there had been a change.

Males are just not as smart as females. I guess they don't have to be since they can usually depend on brute strength. If that had been me, even at that young age, I would have known that My H was attempting a name change. I would have demanded to give my approval. In fact, it was me who came up with my nick-name, Miss Lilly. I like the sound and the feeling of the sound of "Miss Lilly"; it is rolling, soft, and musical.

As mentioned before, we had a habit of putting food and water out everyday so the feral clan could help themselves. One day while on our outing we saw a beautiful guy with long white hair and ice blue eyes had come along and was helping himself to a little food and drink. I was in love instantly. He began coming around a couple of times a day everyday. He obviously was not part of the feral clan so we wondered what his story was and where his human servants were. We never found out because no one in the neighborhood knew anything about him. As we watched him for a day or so, we noticed that every time he tried to swallow, he would stretch his neck long and reach it as high as he could up in the air.

My H made friends with him little by little, and became more and more worried about him as he struggled to eat and drink. While petting him, she found out that he had a flea collar fastened around his neck that he had long ago outgrown. It was so tight around his neck that it was killing him slowly, day by day. He could barely swallow and soon would not be able to breathe. Even though it made the collar tighter for a few seconds, My H managed to get a scissors under it and cut it off of him so he could swallow more easily and not be strangled. We hoped it had not done permanent damage to him but were never sure if it had or not. My H picked him up and brought him into the condo.

Our family had expanded even more. We named him Dreamy Coco because of his beautiful long white fur. Sometime later, My H decided he was an old, wise soul that had taken incarnation as a feline. She said the old, wise soul had a mission to accomplish and could do so from a feline body; she was happy to have relieved that soul from suffering a flea-collar death. At that juncture I didn't know if I believed what she said but it did give me pause to think. He was a rather quiet, contemplative guy and his ice blue eyes did seem to have the wisdom of the ages.

There was a rather unique young man that came around the condo complex everyday who was named "Paper Boy." Odd name, I don't think I ever came across anyone else with that name in all of my long life. He would come around everyday and throw rolled-up newspapers on the ground. When everyone got home from work or play, they would one by one have to pick up those papers off the ground. It was an odd thing for Paper Boy to do. I don't know why no one ever complained or told him to stop littering.

One quiet afternoon we were all sitting on the couch in the living area when it was just about time for Paper Boy to come around. We saw him come by and put the papers on the ground when suddenly there was loud yelling and Paper Boy started pounding on our front door. My H was on her way to open the door and talk to him when all of a sudden we heard very loud popping sounds. Then, we could see an older human male pointing something at Paper Boy; it was making the loud popping sounds. Paper Boy doubled over, dropped all his papers and ran, jumping the back fence. The older human male disappeared in the other direction.

Well, when I looked around to see what My H made of all the commotion, she was nowhere to be seen. She had run into the bedroom to hide and was on the telephone with the police. Those police are supposed to protect us royalty and not allow this type of commotion to occur. In a very short time, the police showed up at the door and took a statement from My H and left.

We never saw Paper Boy any more and I wondered what happened to him. I learned that the older human male had been shooting a gun at Paper Boy, and I could not fathom what would make someone want to hurt him. That unfortunate and frightening incident was the beginning of a stirring in me. I was not pleased, with what was happening in my neighborhood.

Not too long after Paper Boy was shot at, the elderly female human who lived in the house next door to our small condo complex—the house with all the feral cats—died. She did not have family, or friends, or anyone to look after her affairs; in fact, she had never made eye contact, spoken to, or acknowledged any of us who spoke to her or waved at her when she was alive.

For weeks her house just sat there with all of her belongings inside. It was very sad and was not the kind of thing we like to see happen in life. One night when My H came home after dark, she noticed lights on in the empty house and an old white pickup truck parked outside of it. My H called the police and said she thought the house was being burglarized!

About an hour later there was a knock on our door and when My H opened it she saw first one policeman with his gun drawn and pointing in the air, then she saw three more behind him (one was a woman) with their guns pointing in the air. Then she looked the other way and saw four more on the other side of the door with guns pointing in the air.

She said, "I'm the one that called you! I think the house next door is being robbed because the lights are on and there is a truck parked outside. The lady that lived there died and she does not have any family. Why are you here at my door with guns drawn?"

The first police officer said, "Well, there's nobody there now." With that all eight of them turned and left. We were in shock. We just shook our heads and were thankful that we did not have some dire emergency in our condo that had them showing up an hour later. We also said thanks that those eight police at the door didn't shoot us!

My H had several university degrees. She earned three in psychology and two in theology. She was the creative type and became bored if she was only doing one thing. While she had a counseling and psychotherapy practice, she also decided to start a hot-shot delivery service for city-wide deliveries. In the beginning, Grandma was the dispatcher and Two, who was now living with us, was the delivery person. My H found that it cost less for Grandma to take and make calls long distance than it cost to hire someone to dispatch. Later we hired more drivers and a dispatcher, who was handicapped. She could not go to a job everyday, but she could work from home, using the telephone.

Expansion

This delivery service added some excitement and fun to our lives. When the holiday season came around, we got so busy that My H made some of the deliveries herself. One delivery she made was to a law firm.

The order consisted of seven cases each with six champaigne magnums. When she arrived at the law firm, there was only one administrative person in the suite.

Now, these cases were heavy individually and all the more so, with all seven stacked on a handcart. Once inside with the champagne, the lady inside could not decide where she wanted them stacked. Finally, when the cases were all stacked in a neat tower, she wanted them each carried to a separate office. My H said they were too heavy and she could not do that, she was only delivering to the suite, not to individual offices. The law-firm employee said to My H that she had better do what she was told, or she would complain to the owner of the delivery service. My H said, "Here I am, go ahead. Do you want to pay an extra fee for delivery to each office?" That was the end of that.

My H noted to me that people are interesting when they have always felt powerless and then suddenly feel as if they have power. She says they tend to become abusive or suddenly drunk with power. I think that people who work in offices feel superior to people who perform manual labor type work.

The adventures that came from the delivery service added a whole new dimension to our lives. We had a regular midnight Friday-night pick-up from a business, with delivery to the airport, that My H really enjoyed. She and Two would go to a metal-grinding facility to pick up six large, one-hundred-pound pails of grit (ground-up metal) and deliver them to a private dock at the airport. The grit was loaded onto an airplane and delivered to an oil field.

The oil company paid a lot of money to have this service every week. How was that cost effective as opposed to a truck delivering a larger amount of grit once every few months? I don't know, but we were happy to have the account.

One of the guys at the metal-grinding facility was called "Animal" by his coworkers. He never spoke; he would just bark and howl. He was able to follow instructions and do his job but we thought he must not have a place to live. He wore the same dirty, torn jeans and T-shirt all the time; the back of the jeans in the pocket area was torn and hanging down. Animal did not wear underwear. The other guys who worked there said he had inhaled too many chemicals to get high and had done it for way too many years.

Chapter Three
Moving

Again, I digress. People say I do that a lot. Oh, well; it's just who I am. Back to topic. Our smorgasbord, that we put out for the feral cats, attracted a variety of passing royalty over time. One guy that came by several times decided he liked the surroundings and thought he would just stay. One of our neighbors in the condo complex (I called him Neighbor Guy), named this new feline Teddy because he did rather look like a Teddy Bear. Teddy would sometimes spend the night with us, and would sometimes spend the night with Neighbor Guy.

A very short time later Neighbor Guy was shot in the back during an armed robbery as he was waiting for the bus to take him to work early one morning. It was broad daylight on a busy corner just three streets over from where we lived. From then on Neighbor Guy was paralyzed from the waist down. Some said it was a great tragedy that happened for no reason other than he only had $20.00 in his pocket. Others said it was bad karma from the past.

In more recent years, I have come across other ideas that say we draw to us what we give our attention and energy to. So, I don't know, maybe neighbor guy had a lot of fears or negative thoughts? Maybe he was just in the wrong place at the wrong time. And, although his life was certainly drastically altered in an instant, when we came

18

across him a few decades later, he was happy and content with his life. There are many questions that remains unanswered for me.

Three events involving violence in a row, in what had been a peaceful neighborhood? That was it for me. I told My H, "You did not rescue me from that shelter just to have me killed right here at home or left orphaned if they kill you. Get me out of here!"

Thank goodness she listened. She began to think about where we should live. Then an advertisement showing land for sale in a neighboring state just popped up one day. She and Two agreed to buy land, move, and build a house. My H said, "At least one of us has to have a job before we move." They both began searching for jobs and researching types of houses to build. My H found a company not far from the land that provided log-house kits and Two found a job at a hospital. They sold the delivery business and the condo, bought the land, and we were off.

We packed all our belongings into our two pick-up trucks and a van owned by Two's mother, Gloria, and we hit the road. But, not before My H's mother tried to stop us from moving so far away. She sent one of My H's friends to tell us she was in the hospital. When My H called her, she was not in the hospital, she had not even been to the doctor.

Moving

So, we made our move to our new state. We had a very long drive that at some points went over treacherous mountain roads. Two was first in line, then My H with us felines, and then Two's mom in the van. The road was narrow and on the outside of the lane there was a steep drop-off of a couple hundred feet or more.

Before we could get to our new town and off the mountain pass, we still had several hours of driving in the dark and it was raining. Gloria kept running the van right up to the back of My H's truck, so close we could not see her head-lights; this was in the dark as we were going down hill on the steep, wet roads. Later Gloria admitted she did it on purpose hoping to knock My H off the road to stop us from making the move. That could have been deadly. I don't know about human mothers and the lengths they will go to keep their children close to home!

Chapter Four
The Country

We moved far away out into the country just outside of a very small and quiet town. That's where this account began, where we lived with the two smelly beasts outside and the two barn giants, Filoriana and Prince. Our life was good except for the occasional copperhead snake. A darling like me has to be very careful out in the woods, so I had My H come along on all my walks to make sure I was safe.

Later, after I died, she did place my body outside for nature to take its course. But I was free of my body at that point and was not afraid. My guardian angels impressed upon her consciousness how they wanted my body to be handled. She understood that giving my body to nature would free my soul to fly on to the other side faster, and allow me to advance more quickly. She loved me very much and wanted the best for me, even if it was uncomfortable for her. Because of the way she set my soul free, instead of burying me, I am able to come and go easily between earth and heaven.

One time in the quiet and solitude of the country, I heard a human voice racketing the air outside with loud talking. My H went running out and Shaba and I followed. The two outside smelly beasts came running, too. Two, was yelling, "Get the shotgun! There's a copperhead."

My H went running inside and came back lickety-split with the shotgun. Two said, "Shoot it. Hurry up and shoot it!" My H said, "Where is it?" Two said, "Between my legs." My H, "I can't shoot a shotgun between your legs! Stand very still and wait for it to move away from you."

Two continued to shout, "Shoot it, shoot it! I can't stand with my legs like this much longer." My H went closer, bent over and looked very carefully among the leaves and said, "I don't see any snake. I think it has moved on." Two looked down between her legs and said, "It was right there. Shoot it. Shoot right there!"

Well, by that time the snake was long gone; and finally Two moved her legs and walked away. Probably all the yelling scared that snake so much it slithered away in fear of its life. That was a close one for all of us, I tell you!

That wasn't the last we saw of the copperhead clan. We had chickens that lived in a three-sided chicken coop not too far from the barn, and provided eggs for us. They were free-range chickens that could come and go as they pleased around the property. Well, a copperhead took up residence in a corner of the coop. Sneaky snake that it was, it was living in the corner of the wall, not on the ground where anyone would look for a snake. That snake was stealing chicken eggs and Two was afraid it would kill the chickens. So, we had to move the chickens into the barn until such time as the snake could be persuaded to move on.

The humans grabbed the chickens by their feet and moved them into the barn while I supervised and directed. I shouldn't laugh, but it is still funny to this day. Two had a chicken in each hand and was passing within three feet or so of My H when darned if one of those chickens didn't reach out and bite My H on the hand and held on! She could not get loose from that bite and it really hurt. Finally the chicken let go in order to yell some more and she got loose. She had that scar for the rest of her life.

Another time, we found one of the roosters dead near the chicken coop. ... don't know if it was a copperhead, a coyote, or something else that got it. We might not have even noticed the poor thing except those smelly beasts were rolling all over it. They're worse than human heathens.

Oh, tip: if you're human, never wear open-toe sandals while walking around outside in the woods. Not only could a snake get you, or a dangerous insect, but animals can come after you, too! One day, a raccoon came walking right up to Two, bold as you please, reached out, and grabbed one of her big toes. I think that raccoon thought the toe was a grape or a nut or something else edible.

Chapter Five
Some Unique Places

At one point, My H had a private practice office in the country. It was in a lush, green valley just off the main highway outside the town we lived close to. There were running streams throughout that property that fed the thick, bright green grass and beautiful pine trees. She had a one-room building with a "fainting couch" in it, a chair, and a beautiful hand-painted glass etching that Grandma brought back from a vacation in Norway.

The location was very private, and peaceful with the gurgling sound of the streams. Too bad it was in tornado alley. Yep! A tornado came ripping through lifted the building up and smashed it down to the ground. Everything was in splinters except the glass etching. It did not have a scratch. Thankful that the etching made it through and that no one was hurt, My H just started seeing her clients under a large tree outside the grocery store.

During that same storm that created the tornado in tornado alley, another cyclone came roaring right over our log house. It twisted a couple of trees just outside, but it did not do a lick of damage to the house. I think log houses are very strong. Probably as strong as a concrete house, only more vulnerable due to termites.

Sometimes we would go to visit friends in Coza Home. It was really named Cozy Home by the people that lived there, but when the census takers came around in the early 1900s, they misunderstood the local accent and heard "Coza Home." This was a community about four miles off the main two-lane highway that had a population of about one hundred people.

There were homesteads that had existed there for generations. While life revolved around the church and making ends meet with little else to do, people seemed happy. There were beautiful vistas that reached for miles outward and miles downward. Life carried on in Coza Home much as it had for a hundred years or more. Families lived in houses that had been occupied by their parents, grand-parents, and great-grandparents. The only improvements were electricity and running water brought right into the house, and closets turned into water closets (bathrooms).

About an hour and a half farther on down the two-lane highway was Mountain View. This was a lively little town where tourists liked to visit. Every night there was music around the square with guitars, a zither, and singing. Some of it was blue-grass music and some of it was church hymns. All of it was beautiful and uplifting. People would make annual treks to visit Mountain View and crafts people would bring their wares to sell on the side of the road or around the square. The whole area was a scene that could have been from fifty to a hundred years earlier (except for the automobiles and motor-homes).

There were still some homes in this northern part of the state that did not have electricity or running water or even a road leading to them. Notice, I did not say a paved road. There were no roads at all to some houses. The people living in them had never owned an automobile. They had always used horses to come and go.

In fact, there was an elderly couple who were no longer able to care for themselves but insisted on staying in their own home, a home that did not have electricity, or running water, or a road. The problem came when they could not cut firewood anymore or bring water from the creek to the house. They had been just sitting in their house with no food, no water, and no heat when a home-health nurse found them. It was a very sad day when the home-health nurse had to have the sheriff come and force them into his off-road vehicle and take them to the nursing home.

Chapter Six
Grandma's House

Shaba and I were the royal escorts for My H and Two when they traveled. The other royals stayed and looked after the property and house in the country. Every once in a while, we traveled back to the city where I was born; I would always know fifty miles out that we were approaching. I just sensed it. We felines are just gifted that way. Usually, we didn't even stop in that city, though. We'd pass right on through on our way to the coast.

When we would get to the causeway and big bridge that connected the mainland with the island, I could smell the salt air and the sea life living in the Gulf. I always sent My H messages to open the windows of the car so I could whiff in the air full on, nostrils pointed up. I loved the coast, and not just because I knew I would get fresh shrimp. (I haven't said previously, but surely my readers understand that when I talked to My H sometimes I used feline language, but always I used thought transference. Surely, you've understood that.)

The coast is where Grandma lived (My H's mother). She called herself Grandma when she talked to me about herself. It was a quaint human trait. So, I indulged her and called her Grandma, too. Grandma kind of lived in her own world that was parallel to, yet interconnected with, the world the rest of us lived in. She had her own version of things. She would call us felines—me, Shaba and the ones that lived in her house—the "people." She thought that the "people" needed some shrimp every day. Hmmm, maybe I like Grandma's version of reality.

Grandma had a very strong will but was not always able to use it in positive ways. After an automobile accident when the doctors told her she would never walk again, she said, "Oh, yes I will!" And, after a year of physical therapy, she did. Other times she would get into negative thinking and think herself sick.

When she healed from that auto accident, she gave much of the credit to My H who had spent hours and hours laying on hands, directing healing energy to Grandma's legs and broken pelvis. Yet, other times Grandma would say things like My H was no good and had been no good since the day she was born, or even before she was born. Not all of Grandma's world was pleasant. I think Grandma was delusional at times.

Grandma was a funny human. Every time we came to visit, she would greet us at the door with nonstop talking, and would recognize my royal status as she welcomed me. We'd go inside where she had fresh water sitting out for me in my special bowl. I let Shaba drink from it, too. She put out cat food for us and then gave us shrimp.

Later we'd go out into the back yard and explore with our humans on guard duty. There were some really great smells there. The grapefruit trees would drop their fruit on the ground so there were always lots of really great bugs to sniff and pounce on. Did I ever tell you about the time Shaba almost caught a butterfly? Well, that can wait for another time. This is about me.

So, what I really liked about Grandma's back yard was the smell of the bird droppings. They were totally different from the ones anywhere else: they smelled of salt. Even the birds that didn't eat fish had salt in their droppings. I guess it's the salt in the water and in the plants that the saltier water rains down on. Now, the other birds, the ones that did eat fish? Well, their droppings were euphoric because they smelled of fish and other marine life. I really liked leaving my smells in the yard, too, so other felines and other animals could know I was there. It's like saying, "Ha, I was here and you didn't even know it!"

Oh, okay. I'll tell you about the butterfly. It was early one morning at Grandma's when My H was taking us for our first outing of the day. There was a beautiful, large yellow butterfly moving around from rosebush to rosebush. It flew over us several times way up above. When it came by yet again, Shaba flew straight up in the air about five feet from a reclined position. He clapped his two front paws together to try and catch that butterfly. He almost had it. I think the air movement from his paws coming together pushed the butterfly just out of his reach. He came down and landed as gracefully as a feather. I don't know what gets into that guy sometimes!

I'm in a sharing mood, and will let Shaba have the limelight just a bit longer so I can tell you that he saved all of our lives. One morning, we were all asleep at Grandma's when Shaba came up to My H and whacked her on the head with his paw. That was his way of telling her to wake up and let him out. My H had a very hard time waking up. But she did, and she went to the yard door and let me and Shaba out. When she did, she realized that the air inside the house was full of gas.

She awakened Grandma and Grandpa who then shut the gas off, called the plumber, and aired out the house. It was ten o'clock in the morning when Shaba had rescued all of us. We normally would have been up by seven. If it had not been for him we all would have died right there. It's not a bad way to go, I guess, peacefully while sleeping. But it was not our time. We all had much more to accomplish in our earth lives.

Sometimes, when we were visiting Grandma's, My H and Grandma would go shopping. While they were out I would explore around the house. I found all sorts of interesting things. Like what, you wonder? Well, I found discarded wads of hair from

Grandma's cats; I found dried up puddles on the floor from when they were angry with her and did not use their litter box; I found dust balls, and sometimes I found very stiff crunchy bugs that had been under the bed for some time.

As interesting as Grandma's house was, I did start to miss home after a while and wonder about the rest of our feline family, the smelly beasts, and even the barn giants. There always came a time when I was ready to head home. And so I would begin sending My H messages that it was time to go.

As is the way with most humans, she would think it was her idea to get on the road and go home, or she would believe she had pre-planned our departure time. As anyone who knows royal felines will attest, we all know without a doubt that when I said it was time to go, we went.

The trip back to the country was always more relaxed for me, because on the way somewhere I was never sure of where we were going until, say, I could sense that we are approaching the city of my birth, or until I smelled the salt air. On the way back, I knew we were going home. So, I could quietly sleep and dream about the adventures of my waning vacation.

We always had to drive through Little Rock and on up from there. More than once after leaving the city, and before we arrived at the next town, we would be driving along and suddenly with no segue, we would be in a different—yet nearby—place with some unaccountable loss of time. Yes, that is what I said. We would find ourselves several miles back from where we had been, or forty or fifty miles ahead of where we had last been conscious of being. One time, we were even on a different, but nearby, highway, and had to get out the map to figure out how to get back to the highway we needed.

Now, if this had happened to only one person, I'd say maybe she fell into a trance of sorts and was not paying attention to what she was doing. But it happened to all of us, and we all had the same shock and confusion at being in a different location, with no memory of how it happened.

The time was always off, too. Sometimes it was only by ten or fifteen minutes and sometimes it was by hours. Maybe we had just noticed the clock said 10:00 a.m. and suddenly it was 10:45 a.m. and we were in a different location. One time we were about forty miles off course and only one minute had passed. How did time not match distance and how did we get transported?

One time as we became aware of this happening, we noticed a loud thump noise and a jostling of the car. My H said she thought it was aliens abducting us and letting us go. If it was, they never hurt us and we never had any ill effects from it.

Chapter Seven
Rush River

One of the most fun things I would do during the day was to get up on top of the antique, glass-front bookshelf and wait for My H to walk by. When she did, I would whack her on the head and fluff her hair around. We'd laugh and laugh. I think she walked by when I was up there just so we could play this game. I also liked to bat at the lamp that used to hang from the ceiling right there by the bookshelf.

Humans need help to lighten up. We have to remind them to let their inner child play and have fun. Laughing is one of the best medicines; it is right up there with love. Humans are so serious and fearful; do they ever lighten up? No wonder so many of them are depressed. They make their own lives miserable.

I think one reason we felines (and canines, too) have chosen to be companions to humans, is to help them make their lives more enjoyable. I did my best to teach My H to speak feline so we could communicate more clearly and so she could expand her view of the world. There are some concepts I wanted to teach her that can only be understood in the feline language. She needed me to teach her about the royal nature of all of us. Among other things, she needed the experiential knowledge that we are all part and parcel of the One, and that we are not ever victims.

She needed to understand that we have the power to shape our experiences. These things cannot be conveyed adequately by human speech. Helping her to speak feline enabled her to put herself in feline shoes and know that we are all one. I must say, she had some of the more simple sounds down fairly well. She could even make some of the sounds that the feral cats made. Her accent was okay, and she seemed to understand the meaning of the words as well.

I loved my walks out to view and explore our property when we lived in the country. I led the whole family in a line; we looked like a parade. First me, then Shaba and all of the rest of us felines, then My H, then Two, then the horses, and last of all the smelly beasts. We all took family walks around the perimeter of our property. We checked the fences and the vegetation. We did have to be careful of the snakes and scorpions.

One time on our walk we went past one of our property boundaries where a new neighbor had moved in, and I couldn't believe it! They had moved our fence about twenty feet and taken our property. Let me tell you! I sent the humans to get their tools and supplies and we moved that fence right back into place, right then and there! We kept a check on that property line from then on; those greedy people never moved that fence again!

Oh, get this! One time My Human decided she would get some vegetable seeds, and just throw them out on the ground in the forest to see if they would grow. They did not grow. Duh! Humans! She thought this would work because on one part of the property, wild asparagus was growing.

It was close to the creek where I loved to just hang out and be with the wood nymphs. They were all over our property but especially down by the creek. They loved the creek as much as I did. The sight of the crystal-clear water running over the rocks was at least as delightful and pleasing as the sound it made. There is no way to describe that gentle gurgling sound of water seamlessly gliding over and beyond the rounded rocks.

There were moments of heaven on those walks in the country. I guess there are moments of heaven happening frequently in life, if we only let our consciousness notice them. Even the sound of boots or paws walking on snow in a silent winter forest is a bit of heaven. Life is full of beauty; we need only intend to see it.

That is probably a reason traveling is so essential. When we change our perspective, change our scenery, and make time for leisure, we can perceive our surroundings and our reactions much more clearly.

While I rarely went for joyrides in the car, I would always know where My H was, and what she was doing. When she went to the grocery store, I would always impress upon her mind that she should buy cans of cat food, and I would tell her what brands and flavors I wanted. Sometimes I told her to buy a can of tuna for me. She would laughingly acknowledge my mind messages to Two. At first Two, thought My H was a little off her rocker with all of her ESP mumbo-jumbo. Then an incident happened when we were living in the city of my birth.

My H said she could sense a particular neighbor woman spying on us when we would walk or drive past her apartment. My H pointed out the window and said she was spying on all the neighbors with binoculars. Two told her that she was just paranoid. A week later, Two was eating crow, because there was an article in the newspaper about how the woman had called the police on a couple of guys in the apartment across the street from her front window. She wanted the police to arrest the guys for what they were doing in their apartment. When the police asked her how she knew what they were doing in the privacy of their apartment, she admitted to watching them through a crack in their curtains with her binoculars. The police arrested her for peeping on the neighbors.

Okay that was another digression. Back to task. The winters in the county were something else! Cold, cold, cold, and more cold. In the winter it could stay

Fahrenheit twenty-two degrees below zero for days. Deep snow would cover the ground, the main road, the creek, the trucks, the cars, and the fences. Sheets of ice covered the driveway down to the house from the road up above, and the creek would ice over. Ice collected everywhere, hanging from the roof of the house like daggers waiting to fall. I was never so glad to live inside in my life! Well, you know I was born on the southern coast and never did adjust to those cold winters.

After a really harsh winter, spring had finally arrived when we heard about some kittens that lived in a barn on a neighbor's property; the neighbors were cattle ranchers. We found out that the poor little orphans had lost their mother and had to be bottle-fed. So, when they could eat solid food, we went and got them and brought them to live with us. There were two of them.

We named them Sunkist (alias Miss Meepy) and Kali (Alley Kat Kay). Sunkist was a cute little girl with fur of yellow and orange stripes (i.e., Sunkist) and Kali was a beautiful little girl with fur of a tortoise-shell mixture of colors. The "Miss Meepy" part of the name came along a little later and signified the fact that Sunkist could not meow. She could not make any noise at all except for purring, and the sound her lips made when she tried to say meow. It sounded like "Meep." Hence, Miss Meepy.

When we first brought those two kittens home they were wild children. They had hardly any socialization, and no schooling at all. When we brought them home and let them out, they went and hid in an old hollowed-out tree just beyond the front of the house. They refused to come out, and we had to just feed them in the log and put a dish of water in there for them. I went and talked to them; Shaba went and talked to them. We rubbed on the tree and meowed to them. Nothing! They said we didn't know what we were talking about; they said humans smelled and did their business inside and were loud and scary.

They had lived in the hollow tree for about a day when it started to rain, and kept on raining and raining hard. My H was very concerned about those little kittens—she thought they might drown out there. She went out in the rain, put her hand down into that old hollowed out tree, grabbed those kittens up and brought them inside. She didn't let them back out for a week. By then, they decided that living inside with the rest of us was not so bad after all and they never went far off on their own again. They were allowed to go out exploring and enjoying the insects but always came back for dinner from then on.

These two were not the last felines to join our family. One day Two came home from her job with the cutest little grey kitten. She was born on a ranch in another town and needed a home. She could not see much into the distance so we called her Charlie

Sue Magoo (Magoo, like the nearsighted cartoon character). Her alias was Baby Goo.

I have to tell you about the Rush River and what we found there. It is a magical place and possibly the most beautiful place I have ever seen. To get to it, you can only drive so far and then you have to walk the rest of the way. (There were many places like that in the northern part of the state.) Where we liked to go visit was where the river converges with one of its larger tributaries. There were some people—a woman and a man with a young son— who hand-built a home out of felled trees, right where the river and tributary converge. They cut and shaped the trees by hand, and stripped them to build their house. While it is beautiful and magical, it was not wise to build there. It floods.

One of the things that makes it a magical place is the constant music of the flowing water. You can barely hear anything else. That water is crystal clear and as sweet as if you mixed it with sugar. In the spring, you can't go anywhere near the center of the river, and certainly can't cross it. With all the melting snow swelling the river it just isn't safe. There are rocks there under the water, and when the water rushes over them in the spring it must be going at least twenty miles per hour. The sound can be deafening.

We were there in the fall one year—the air was chilly already but there wasn't any snow on the ground yet. My Human went wading into the now-slower-moving tributary, and as she was looking around something glimmering more than the water caught her eye. She reached down and pulled out a very large crystal.

This crystal was so unusual! It was still attached to about six inches of rock comprised of grey sparkly layers compressed together. That was unusual in itself, but even more unusual, I think, is that at the top the crystals were worn down smooth. There were no jagged edges, it was just flat. Or, semi-flat: there was a step-down and a lower part of the crystal face on one side. It was a gorgeous piece of rock crystal and none of us has ever seen anything like it to this day. Water is so soft and yet so powerful. I am still amazed that water could wear the long pointed crystals down to a flat surface.

Chapter Eight
Freedom

First Shaba died and then within a year, I died. At least that is what My H called it, death. She was very sad when I died. She loves me very much. She thought that I was gone, but I was still right here. Only now I was free of any restrictions; I could go with her everywhere she went. I didn't have to stay at home when she went out in the car. Sometimes I tried to let her know, "I am here", but she was not too good at perceiving me. After Shaba died that summer, he just felt like staying on the other side and enjoying himself. He did not visit with My H very often.

If I want to, I can go back to anytime in my lifetime to visit and watch. I can even attempt to influence my past-self, the humans, felines, and the others. Of course, they all have free will and can ignore my promptings. After I died, I would still tell My H what to do, and help guide her through life. As always, she believed her thoughts and decisions were her own. My job is an unrecognized labor of love.

Anyway, not too long after I died, I could see that the extreme cold in the country was not good for My H's health so I suggested to her that she move to a warmer climate. She decided to move to a smaller city in our original State. Ushuti Two Shoes, Dreamy Coco, Sunkist (alias Miss Meepy), Kali Alley Kat

Freedom

Kay and Charlie Sue Magoo rode in the truck with My H for the move. The smelly outside beasts rode in the other truck with Two. The two horses went to new homes and the log house and forty acres went to new owners.

With the move to the house in the small city, the felines had much exploring to do. When My H would go to work, everyone set about the business of finding all the smells, all the bugs' hiding places, that sort of thing. My life in the new house was a total joy, as I did not have a solid body ('meat body' is what I call it). In my afterlife body, I can go as high as I want with no fear of falling, move right through walls, never have a pain or an itch, never feel hungry. I can smell up all the food I want and never feel too full and I don't have to go to the vet for exams or get shots. Life after life is good.

Ushuti Two Shoes always liked to do her own thing; I think it was her feral roots. When we moved to the small city, she started doing yoga. Have you ever seem a feline do yoga? It might be one of the most beautiful things anyone could ever see. We had a long mantle that lined the wall, running from the living area around the open doorway into the dining room. Two Shoes would glide up to that ledge so gracefully that she really looked as if she were flying. Once up there she would do her stretches and bows and deep breathing. Then she would walk from one end to the other and back again. The thing is, she would do it in slow motion.

She was doing a walking meditation like they do at Buddhist meditation retreats. I've never seen anything like it. I just can't do it justice in trying to describe it. She would slowly, slowly lift one paw at a time, move it ever so slowly forward, slowly shift her weight, slowly place the paw down again, then here comes the next paw so slowly beginning to lift and shift. She could take an hour at a time for this walking meditation. We couldn't put any decorations on the mantle; she had it claimed for her meditation and yoga.

After we lived in this house a while, Ushuti Two Shoes died of blood clots stuck in her heart. From time to time, Two Shoes does visit from the other side, and My H seems to sense her presence, and mine. Not too long after Two Shoes let go of her earth body, Dreamy Coco died too. He just stopped eating one day. The vet gave My H some medicine for him, but he would not swallow it. She tried to get him to eat but he would not. Before he could go back to the vet, he just died. The quality of his passing seemed different from the rest of us and he is not with us felines and canines on the other side, so maybe he really was a special soul and has gone on to a more advanced plane on this other side. I don't know.

It was around this time that I first let My H see how we live on the other side. I wanted to help her know that we are not only doing well, but that we have a great life and are very happy and very well cared for. We have all manner of toys and tunnels to climb in and run through. We can climb as high as we want and fly across the room. We never fall, or get hurt, or have hair balls or any of those earthly inconveniences. We just play and groom and love life (life after life that is). We do have some learning sessions too, but we have fun. It is all play, relaxation, and enjoyment, even when we are learning.

Chapter Nine
Think It And It Is So

Over here on the other side, if we think a thing, it is. We can create anything or any experience we choose. True, that is no different than it is on the "alive" side where you are, except that here it is much quicker and easier. It is also less "permanent" over here. On this side, we can change anything, any time, instantaneously, with just a thought. Over there on your side, you have to sustain a thought and the belief in your ability to manifest for a long time of highly focused concentration, with feeling and intention to bring change or to manifest.

I think the major difference is in your belief system. When you actually believe you can bring something into being, you do. To me, it is like the difference between easily gliding through air like a feather, or trudging through nearly frozen mud with weights pulling you down.

Over here when I want to travel to see an old friend, say, a human that I know who has come to this side, like Grandma, I just think of being in her company, at her house, or of being with her out by a lake, and, wham, there I am. If I want to be with My H who is still on the living side, I just intend to be there with her and "insto-presto," there I am. If I want to romp with Shaba, Dreamy Coco, or Ushuti Two Shoes, I just send them a thought invitation and here they are, arriving for some great playtime.

I have many lessons to learn over here because I have an opportunity to return to your side as a human next time. When I first talked to my guides and guardians about separating from the group soul and moving into the human-soul range, my review showed that I already know about self-confidence, love, loyalty, and continuity of experience both within a lifetime and between lives. I have to learn other things like compassion, goal setting, flexibility, and sustained intention. I already have the under-standing of, and intention of, verbal communication, so that when I am in my human body, I shouldn't have any difficulties learning to manipulate sounds into words with intention and positive results.

What I don't understand is, if this whole living thing is a paradigm we all set up to have a play-ground for experiences, and if we can change any part of it at any time to suit our desires, what is the reason for taking it all so seriously? I see that My H and other humans worry about everything constantly. Even those who seem to be on the fringes of society take their rebellion or their outcast status very seriously. They seem to be very unhappy, but don't seem to do anything to change their situation in the game of life.

I digress. My guardians and I are considering that I might be a writer in my first human life. I will probably be a female again since it is more currently familiar to me and I will have to deal with so many other changes and new experiences, no need to add one more. I wanted to take birth into the family with My H, but she is not going to have any children in the future of her life, so my guardians and I are looking for the right mom for me. I don't know if I will be born into a family or just to a couple or just to my mom. I have to wait and see what appropriate situation we can find for me.

In the meantime, there is so much to consider, to learn, and to practice. For example, as a human, I will not be allowed to lap up my milk from a bowl. I will have to use my hands to hold a vessel. First I will suck from a nipple to get my milk, then use a small plastic cup, and finally drink out of a glass. To make matters even more confusing, there are mugs to drink from, disposable plastic cups, cans, bottles of glass or plastic, and who knows what else that humans drink from at various times. Some people drink soup from a bowl. My guardian says not to worry, that my human mom will teach me, and I will have teachers at school. She says just by being alive as a human, I will learn their ways.

My intention in choosing to live a human life is to be of more help, and assist the life wave advancement. I don't think that humans are superior to felines just because they have opposable thumbs and larger brains. The thumbs would be useful to have, but in my opinion, the larger brain thing is just a result of having a larger body. If a feline brain has more folds and a more intricate structure than a larger human brain that has few if any folds, which is the more intelligent brain? I think we have to consider this question on a case-by-case basis. There may be some humans with superior intellect but in general, I do think felines are vastly superior.

To prove my point, a superior species would be the one who is served by another species, don't you think? Who serves who, here? Humans serve and care for felines. They obtain our food and present it to us; also, they tend to our waste disposal and our health needs. They entertain us and present us with toys, treats, and gifts. Who is the servant here and who is served? I rest my case.

Chapter Ten
Seeing Clearly

It was time to move again. This time we were going back to the mountains in yet another state. It would be cold again, but I didn't care because I didn't have a "meat body." So, now it was just My H, Two, Sunkist, Kali, and Charlie Sue Magoo who made the move, along with the two smelly beasts.

I told My H to seek out beauty in our new home and she did. The new scenery was breath-taking. It was like living in a picture postcard everyday. That's what Two said. We took rides and long walks just to see the beauty. Sunkist and Kali stayed home and watched the house. My H and I could sit at her desk in the house and look out the window while she worked, and watch the deer standing and nibbling at the ground among beautiful pine trees. Sometimes there was white, icy snow on the ground every-where. Often we would go for hikes along the South Fork River; I loved it best where there was snow on the ground and the only thing I could hear was each crunchy foot-step.

These river walks were magnificent. We walked through pine groves, crossed open fields of flowers or snow blankets depending on the time of year; we traversed logs to cross the river several times; we saw rock ledges; we walked on rock ledges; we saw outcroppings of rocks along the river; we swam in a natural pool made by the rocks where the water is ice cold as it runs down the mountain toward the river; we hiked and hiked, until we finally had to head back home. There was nothing else like it in life.

Toward the beginning of our river hike there was an old perimeter foundation from someone's used-to-be home. There was still part of a chimney there, and if we looked inside, we could see where the floor used to be. My H was fascinated with this old homestead. She believed she knew the story of the people who used to live there. According to her, there was a woman who had four small children and tended sheep and kept chickens. She had a garden patch and knew how to find herbs, flowers, leaves and bark from the forest for medicine, spices and flavored teas. She would fish and would sell the fish for money. After a while she bought a cow with the fish money.

The woman had a husband who was gone hunting or trading most of the year. When he came back, he would always bring some honey as a treat for the family. They had a horse, but the man usually took it with him, so the woman and her children had to walk wherever they went. Other traders would come by from time to time, and in the spring the woman would take the children and walk to visit neighbors. They would stay for several days during the visit and then walk home. Once, a trader with a wagon gave them a ride most of the way home.

Somehow the woman stopped living and so did her children. My H thinks it was an illness that got them. She says that even before that, one of the boy children hit his head on a rock while swimming and never came up for air again. She says that when the man came home the last time from hunting and found his family dead, he left and never returned.

What My H was not aware of, as far as I know, is that she could discern all of this information about the people who used to live in the house because they were still there. At least their energy is still here. As she talked about the family and what used to be, I could see everything she was saying because they have left energy traces behind. I could see them in their daily activities, walking to the river, eating, getting sick, going under water and not coming back up—all of it. It was like watching a movie that was faded and had a newer, brighter movie being recorded over it. Both are still there, the old one was just harder to see. You really had to settle in and be quiet to be aware of it.

My H said there used to be Native Americans who roamed these woods also. She's right; I could see them. She said there were several villages not too far away and that she could still feel their energy, know some of their thoughts, and feel their wisdom. She said the river was central to all sentient beings in the area and sustained all human, animal, and plant life. What I know is that it is not just the water from the river physically maintaining life, it is the energy, the vibrational song of the river that enlivens and permeates everything for miles around. I could see the colors flowing off the river in waves and spreading into the distance like waves on the ocean.

Chapter Eleven
Timberline

Sometimes we would go for drives in a different direction. I loved to go visit Timberline. While the river was magical for its beauty and energy, Timberline was earthy. It had no pretense and no striving. It was remote!

On the way to Timberline we had to pass through an Indian Reservation that was a mysterious place in many ways. My H had to drive through it on the way back and forth to her job; there were strange things that happened on that highway. For example, there was an old-fashioned red car that always had four people in it, that would repeatedly appear out of nowhere in the same place on the highway, at about the same time of day. It did not happen all the time, just sometimes. When I say out of nowhere, that is what I mean. There were no roads joining the highway at that location; the view was clear; there were no trees at that spot: there was no explanation. The car with the people in it would just appear on the highway, traveling at highway speed and go on down the road. Sometimes the car would materialize in front of My H and sometimes in back of her. It would drive on ahead and out-of-sight.

Timberline sits on a mountain top, and at that time electricity had not reached that far. It was the most beautiful and quiet place I have ever experienced. It even rivals what I have created for myself over here on the other side as far as peacefulness and sheer beauty. The tree-arched road off the highway to Timberline was not paved, and when there was snow on the ground or when the snow has just melted, it could be quiet a challenge to get there. The whole drive there was one moment of beauty after another. We would see trees up close, then far-away vistas, then nothing but a curving blanket of trees as we made a hairpin turn up the mountain. Then we would see another open vista where we were on the edge of the road, teetering on the side of the mountain. Two would say, "What do you see?" Then My H would say, "...down." They would say the same thing every time and then they'd laugh. Humans! So predictable.

Other times we would just go and sit next to the river right in town, just to listen to it and bask in its relaxing energy. It is a very loud river. I guess that's why they call it Rio Ruidoso. The water comes rushing over the rocks at a very fast pace and makes so much noise it is hard to hear what anyone is saying. Maybe that's why it was so relaxing. No one can just jabber on; they all have to be quiet. Is that what meditation is? It reminds me of a miniature Rush River, where we had found the smoothed-down crystal when we lived in the country.

Other times we took a longer drive to the north where we would see one vast lake after another. Those lakes had crystal-clear blue water, and were so large there was no way to see from one side to the other. When one lake ended, very shortly another huge lake just like the one before came into view.

To the East we would take drives until there was no more road. Then have to walk into where we wanted to go. We would walk along a narrow river that had beaver dams. On one side of our path was the wall of a high hill and on the other side was the river. There was lush vegetation everywhere. So much beauty and solitude! There's nothing like it. Surely the isolation is what kept it pristine.

Contrast that to the drives we would take South, where there are stretches of land that seemed like desert. There was a dusty town called Zinc where there used to be zinc mines and where the people lived a very simple and peaceful life. My H and Two had friends in Zinc that they used to go visit; the lady would serve cherry pie that she'd made. She reminded me of Grandma a little except that this lady was very sad. She had survived the holocaust as a child and had tried to put her past behind her. But when the newly-elected head of a hate organization moved to Zinc, a whole entourage of followers moved in, too. They were very nasty and caused constant trouble, almost for the fun of it, it seemed. Our friends moved away from Zinc and so did everyone else from the original community. They just abandoned their homes and land and headed away for safety.

Chapter Twelve
Grandma Went Floating

A hurricane came and nearly wiped everything off the island where Grandma lived. She wasn't there, because she had the sense to leave before the hurricane hit. She came with her three felines and stayed with My H. It's a good thing because the water would have gotten her.

The wonderful house with all the grapefruit trees, and insects on the ground, and butterflies, and rose bushes—it was all flooded with over four feet of salt-water. Everything in the yard died and the house was a mess with mold and dirt. It smelled very bad and Grandma could not go back to live in it. Grandpa had already come over to this side the year before. So, Grandma had to get an apartment in an assisted-living building in the city of my birth, across town from where My H was living. It was quite a change for Grandma, but she managed to adjust. She did well for a while, then a process seemed to start. I think it was because of a thought that became a belief for Grandma.

I think by seeing the elderly people at the apartment building, seeing them age, seeing them lose ground mentally, seeing them being forgetful, seeing them die one by one over time, and hearing them express their belief in old age, deterioration, and dying, Grandma came to believe in aging and death. She had been vibrant and active before the hurricane, but she became less active, did not eat as healthfully, and began saying things like, "Oh, I'm becoming just like the rest of them." She forgot that what a person says, manifests. She forgot to be careful about what she placed after "I am."

Grandma could not remember things as well as she used to. Sometimes, she kind of thought My H worked for her instead of being her daughter. She had started having mini-strokes. She didn't let it get her down, though. She kept active by keeping plants on the balcony of her apartment. Funny thing is though, she started to like desserts. She had never been a sweets eater, but now she began eating two and three desserts at a meal. The brain is an interesting thing. It is kind of like the computer of the body, I think. The programming in her computer seemed to change with her changed beliefs, and the strokes physically changed her brain so that some of her memory got wiped.

One day, My H and Two went to visit Grandma in her apartment. There was nothing unusual or eventful about the day, and after a short shopping trip they left Grandma, as she said she was going to lie down and take a nap. My H and Two went to visit a friend who had an orange tree that was full of beautiful ripe oranges. After they filled a couple of bags and were driving off, My H called Grandma to see if she wanted some oranges. Grandma did not answer her cell phone. My H thought that was unusual, but they went ahead on down the road and she called again about ten minutes later. There was still no answer and so My H called the front desk of the apartment building and had them go and check on Grandma. They then headed back to Grandma's apartment.

By the time My H got to the building, an ambulance was there. When she got to Grandma's apartment, she found her on the bed partially sitting up but non-responsive. Several of the employees of the assisted-living facility and the EMTs—the Emergency Medical Technicians—were talking to her. Grandma had to go to the hospital.

In the hospital, she got a little better and could respond, but not talk, or write, or walk. It had been a stroke that had gotten her when she was taking a nap in her apartment. Grandma always had an iron will and without any spoken word, it was obvious to My H and to me that she was determined to recover and go on with her life. Until one of her doctors came into the room one day and began talking to My H in front of Grandma about her never recovering and having to go into a nursing home.

Grandma had come to love her apartment and she was fiercely independent. She knew many of the people living in the apartment building, and had known many of them on the island, the city of My H's birth, for many decades. She had made new friends as well. Upon hearing that she would have to go to a nursing home and never be able to return to her apartment, Grandma became agitated and tried her best to talk as she cried. She was unable to communicate. She could not speak or write, but she could hear and she could process information. Hearing that she would never be able to be independent again made her angry and depressed. We could see it on her face. I was lying next to her on the bed trying to comfort her. It was at that moment that she made up her mind to leave her earth life. Within a few days she did.

My H, Two, and I were with her when she left her body. Very slowly over a few hours her breathing became slower and more shallow. We could see that her body was slowly shutting down. While her body was still coming to a close, we saw her Spirit or Life Force exit her body from the area around her forehead and the top of her head. We could see that she was still in the room with us, watching what was unfolding, even after she left her body. We were there to hold her body's hand and touch her arm lightly. My H brushed her hair gently with her hair brush. Eventually, Grandma's body stopped functioning completely, and Grandma's Life Force went floating out of the room close to the ceiling. So, now she is over here on this side with me.

Chapter Thirteen
Changing Perspectives

While living in this most beautiful and interesting place, Kali developed kidney problems and left her earth life. So, the next move, which was to the coast and the town where My H was born, saw a much smaller family. Now it was just Miss Meepy, Charlie Sue Magoo, the two smelly beasts, My Human, and Human Number Two.

While living in the town of My H's birth, Miss Meepy developed mouth cancer and left her earth life. Charlie Sue Magoo and the two smelly beasts were now the only four-legged ones left in the family. Of course there was always me guiding the family and keeping them safe. After a short stay on the coast, Two got a job in a town a couple of hours away and the family moved again. This time it was to a small country town without much scenery and a lot of quiet.

My H got a job at a newspaper, which was really fun for me. I would go with her to that job; there was so much to learn. I went to work with her everyday, and sniffed around learning the incoming news. I loved seeing how articles are written, where ideas come from, and how advertisements are set. The coins that were collected in newspaper sales had to be sorted, rolled, and taken to the bank. Once one of the newspaper's coin-counters was rude to My H, so I flicked her stacks of coins with my nose and bumped them over. It was with great glee that I observed her consternation at how the coins could just topple over.

There are so many aspects to newspaper work; it is exciting from daybreak to late into the night. Flitting from one place to another, helping where I could, it made me exhausted by the end of the day. I liked most of it, but I seldom hung out with the ones selling advertising over the telephone. That was just plain boring to me.

While we lived in this small town, Two got cancer and came over to the other side to be with all of us four-legged ones. We were all very glad to see her and we play with her all the time. It did make me stop and think. I just don't understand how come all of us, me included, think we have to have a reason, an excuse to leave an Earth life. If we're ready to go, ready to change perspectives, how come we can't just say, "Gotta go. Love ya. See ya later."?

Actually, I do know. We have to create something seemingly beyond our control that forces us to leave our earth life, because the ones who love us would say, "No! Not yet!" "Don't go and leave me here!" "I'm coming with you!" And, so on. So we find an excuse, a disease, an accident; then we are blameless and have no guilt about leaving.

My H was very sad after Two died, so she moved back to the city of my birth with just Charlie Sue

Magoo and the two smelly beasts. Of course, those smelly things had lived outside for quite some time and as indoor dogs they had to get baths regularly. They had become inside dogs once we moved from the country.

For me life in the big city was boring. It was all about driving a long way to get to a boring job, and hurrying to drive a long way home every evening to care for Charlie and the dogs. Faithful companion that I am, I went to work with My H everyday of that tiring and tedious time. As one might guess, eventually Charlie and the dogs came to their time to join us on the other side. My H was all alone (except for me).

She went on this meditation retreat that lasted two months. Now, that was interesting. Those humans would sit on zafus (pillows) on top of cushioned pads for hours at a time and try not to move. I would go around rubbing on them to see if I could tickle them. Then I would reach up, stretching myself up onto their bodies and tickle their faces with my whiskers. I think they did feel it because they would wriggle around and finally rub wherever I tickled them. I know, I know, but I just couldn't help it. They were such easy targets for fun. The retreat leader was a meditation master. I don't know exactly what that means, but I think it means he could let me tickle him and not have to move around or scratch. It was so much fun! When they would get up to do a walking meditation, I would walk with them in line right behind My Human.

What is the purpose of sitting still everyday for two months? I heard talk about seeing clearly, getting clear, centering, reaching enlightenment. Then there was talk of enlightenment taking several lifetimes but some can do it faster. Earlier in life, I had attended yoga classes with My H and heard talk about being a hollow bamboo and observing from the back of the eyes instead of from the front. Well, I must say, that I did see people who had been very tense or very caught up in their personal dramas, become calm and more empathetic. They seemed to focus on themselves less and take a wider perspective.

Now, the drive up to that retreat was fast and My H and I did it all alone. It only took three days from the bottom of the USA to the very top of the USA. On the drive back we brought another human with us who had been at the retreat and we did some sight-seeing and camping out. When we arrived back home, our companion caught a plane and flew to her home state. I think all of us were permanently and deeply changed in ways we did not even conceive of at that time.

Chapter Fourteen
Hurricane Carla

Quite a while before I was born into my royal feline body, My H was still a child living at home with her parents, when Hurricane Carla hit the island where they lived. Before I go on with telling this event, I already know what you will ask. "How can you know what My H experienced before you were even born?"

I'm glad you asked. I'll tell you. Consciousness, awareness, knowing, a sense of self, does not begin and end with the birth or death of a corporeal body. This is one of the reasons I am going to take human birth. It will be my mission to assist others in understanding this concept.

Hurricane Carla hit the island full force, with the eye passing directly over. The family lived in a very strong brick house with a two-foot solid concrete foundation on the high side of the island, and the house was only about six years old at the time of the hurricane. So Grandpa (the father of My H) decided the family could stay home and "ride out" the storm. As I go back and live through the experience from My H's perspective, it was a terrifying event that imbued one with a sense of helplessness. Once the storm was upon them, whatever happened, there was nothing to do but let it play itself out. At the same time, My H did not feel panic, and was prepared to die if that was what was going to happen.

The storm was so violent that no one could talk loudly enough to be heard over it. The 190-mile-per-hour winds shook the house and rattled every window. Even the roof was huffing and puffing, up with a whoosh and down with a thump. It went on for hours, all night long. The house was only four blocks or so from the city's hospital, so when the power went out, the hospital's auxiliary generators extended power to the house. Grandma said it was not right to use the hospital's power, it was needed for the patients and emergencies. So the family only used candles and flashlights all night long. When the eye of the hurricane came directly over the island, it was early morning and full daylight.

The damage to the house was minimal, so Grandpa decided to take the family for a drive in the car to see how the city had fared so far. He knew they only had a brief window of time before the "dirty" side of the storm—the stronger side—would hit. Grandma made the children wear coats even though it was warm outside. There was a stillness all about and an eerie calm, even though there was still a strong wind. My H was rather young and did not weigh much, so that when she was too hot in her coat and opened her coat to cool off, the wind puffed into her open coat sides and lifted her right up off the ground. Thankfully the wind threw her right into a tree that was on the side of the house by the driveway. When she hit the tree at only about three feet off the ground, her arms fell to her sides and the flaps of her coat closed. Without wind in her sails she fell and hit the ground with no harm done.

As the family progressed down the streets they saw that there was debris all over everywhere, and Grandpa had to drive slowly and carefully to avoid disaster. He gave Grandma the 35-mm. camera and told her to take pictures, which she did. (He did not tell her to take the lens cap off.) On the seawall, the waves were still hitting about a foot from the top with such force that they would shoot straight up into the air and arch over the four-lane street, landing on the opposite side on the buildings. The water was not just hitting the seawall and splashing onto the road: after it hit the buildings on the opposite side of the street, it would then splash back across at street-level towards the gulf. The calm of the eye was only relative, not absolute. Everything was still churning out in the Gulf.

Since this was rocking the car about and seemed too dangerous even to Grandpa, he headed away from the seawall toward the heart of the city to see what had happened to it so far. Nearly everything was leveled. The older mansions made of concrete and blocks of rock were standing, but the wood-frame houses and buildings were leveled. One frame hotel was standing, but the storm had ripped the whole side of the building off so we could see right into the rooms, and all the people who had been in those rooms were gone. The storm had sucked them out, blown them away, and washed them right out. Furniture and appliances and corpses were piled everywhere. No one could even begin to think of rescue yet, since the rest of the storm was imminent. There was also no one to rescue, because everything they saw had been underwater for hours. No one and no thing was alive in this part of town.

The family had to go back to their house and live through the rest of the storm. It was louder and stronger, but the house stood and it eventually ended. The family never stayed on the island for another hurricane.

It is not an intelligent thing to do. No one can fully predict the strength of a hurricane or what damage will be done. Humans: do not put yourselves in the path of a hurricane. Escape before it hits and take every pet and other animal you can with you as you go. The propensity for humans to think they can outsmart the force of a hurricane is one of the reasons I don't believe humans to be superior to felines. No feline would voluntarily look a hurricane in the eye, so to speak.

Chapter Fifteen
Not the Usual

Okay, now here's the thing: My H said that during Hurricane Carla she had a vision of the souls lifting up from the earth and moving upward in the sky. She said they were rising out of their bodies, that were dead or dying from being drowned or crushed under the debris. She said she saw a large amount of souls at one time, and then a lesser amount, and then another surge of souls, and then it was over. She said that some years later she saw a painting someone had made of this very scene, except that it was of the 1900 storm. Seeing this painting affirmed for her that what she saw was typical of what happens in mass disasters, and that many people probably see the souls rising.

My H was delighted that she did not see one single soul going down or in any direction but up. She said the painting she saw showed the same thing. She reasoned that since not every person passing out of earth life during the disaster could be perfect, that every soul must get to go to heaven.

What I have learned since that time is that each soul goes to the after-life they picture, and it is based on what they believe. So that if people torture themselves with guilt, do not believe they can be saved and picture a hell for themselves, that is what they will experience. If people picture themselves being with their loved ones in a place very similar to what they had during their earth life, only happier and healthier, then that is what they will experience. If people believe that they will meet great teachers and learn and advance in knowledge, then that is what they will find in heaven. Some people believe that they will be immediately reborn and that is what happens for them. I have learned that heaven has various vibratory levels, just like earth life.

My H said that the land under the house on the island that she lived in from age five had been under water and was part of the Gulf Stream bed at one time, before they brought in fill and extended the island. She said that it had been a shallow sandbar where many ships had run aground, and many people had died there. She would see and hear these tortured spirits as a child and teenager. She could hear them speaking their various languages. Some were angry and menacing and some were very frightened and some were sad; all of them were trapped and felt helpless. Their souls had not ascended when they died. She said other people could see them as well; the house and land were haunted.

What she came to realize was that she could just tell them outright that they were dead, had died in a shipwreck and needed to seek the brightest, whitest light they could find. She would tell them mentally to follow the tunnel to get to the light. She said they all took her advice, some sooner than others, and then were gone.

My H said she had used those same skills and knowledge later in life, when she was in her twenties. She said there had been a young woman, a few years younger than herself, who had been one of a group of friends of hers, and who had died tragically and violently. On the day of the funeral, the group of friends gathered and gave thoughts and prayers for the young woman, Marjorie. My H could feel Marjorie in the room and feel her confusion. She didn't know what had happened to her, didn't know she was dead, and didn't know what to do. My H told the group what she was perceiving and asked that they all mentally let Marjorie know she was dead and needed to go to the light. They did and she did and peace filled the room.

Back to the house where My H grew up. One time, before I came into the family, she and Shaba were visiting Grandma and were sitting in the den while Grandma was in the kitchen cooking. Shaba was sitting on My H's lap when they both saw a dark energy form float at ceiling level from the den into the garden room. Grandma was standing in the kitchen and did not see the dark form, but she was looking at My H and Shaba and saw their heads move in unison as they watched the dark figure move from one room to the other. Grandma asked My H what they were watching and became frightened when she heard. My H said she had seen a dark form float at ceiling level from one room to the other. Grandma said she had seen both My H's and Shaba's heads moving together, watching something she could not see herself, and Grandma started to panic. But My H said there was nothing frightening or sinister about the dark figure—it had been separated from its physical body and was now lost and confused.

It is these types of events that lead me to want to be a human in my next life, so I can help enlighten humans about the different aspects of being, and the energetic, vibrational nature of all of existence. If people understood that life is a continuum, that we are all energy taking different forms at different times, that some of these forms are physical bodies and some are not, then they would understand it is okay to let go after the death of their body. I want all sentient beings to know that they need to look for the brightest light they can find as they are separating from their physical bodies, so they can travel the tunnel and move on to the other side. They need to know to move on.

That leads me to wonder how it is that humans can ever believe that what they see is all there is. There is so much more to life. Just think about the world of the atom with all of its activity and life force. Then think about the world of the heavens, such as galaxies and interstellar space. There is just so much we are not generally aware of; most of us focus on one tiny aspect of the material plane. Isn't it amazing that the world of the galaxies, the world of outer space is the mirror image of quantum space, the world of the atom and the quark? Even more amazing is that the farther we are able to see into the smallest and into the largest, we find repeating patterns, and whatever it is all made from is our Source, and we are all of the same Source.

Personally, I favor the fractal paradigm to explain the phrase from metaphysics that states, "As above, so below." Everything in nature, in living beings, in outer and inner space, takes the same forms and shapes, and all move in the same patterns, all display by the same "rules." How has that come to be?

Another thing I don't understand is how humans can believe that they are separate from everyone and everything else. When a person can feel in alignment with a religion, a philosophy, a metaphysical belief, or some branch of science, they seem happier, more peaceful. Those people who ascribe to only what they see based on their own core beliefs seem to be the loneliest, the angriest, the most fearful, the most isolated of all the humans.

The other sentient beings don't have this type of problem. For example, we felines know that we are part of the whole, we see the energy flows, we feel the magnetism of the earth, we hear the music of the heavens. The same is true for the rest of what the humans call the animal kingdom, and for the plant kingdom and for the mineral kingdom. Just as each cell in the human body has consciousness and a type of thinking, so does a mountain, a tree, a fish. Humans say they are more intelligent, have more capacity to think, have larger brains, but they are also more out of touch with most of existence.

There came a time in life when My H decided she wanted to live on the other side, that is, over here with me. She lives in a house with Two that they made with their thoughts. They go to classes to learn about the laws pertaining to All, and to learn to use thoughts as the mechanism of creation. They are becoming more artistic with their thought-creating. We felines and the smelly beasts can be with them any time we or they want, and we can be with our caretakers when we want, and we can be on our own, playing and learning when we want. This is a very safe and happy place over here.

For me, it is not to be forever. I know that not all beings choose to be reborn into an earth life, but all of us in our group will be coming back over to your side for more lives. Some of us will be there soon and some of us will wait a while. I will probably be the first of us felines to return to your side because of my upcoming life as a human. I'm not sure which of the family members will take birth with me or what our configuration will be. Will My H take birth and then become my mother when I am reborn?? I don't know yet. Will one of the other felines take birth and be my pet, or mom's pet? I think as a human child I would even like to have one of the smelly beasts take birth and be my pet. I think human children are like that.

My H once made a comment about having moved so many times in her life, and how different life was while living in different locations. She said it was like living many lives in one. She said something about the changing of the ages from Pisces to Aquarius, and something about an accelerated rate of karmic cleanup. Maybe I'll be learning more about that sort of thing in my pre-incarnation studies. Anyway for now, I will be concentrating on the things I most need to learn for my upcoming human life, and I'll spend time with my guardians and guides deciding what my life plan will be. I heard something about Two being one of my guardian angels during my earth life.

Chapter Sixteen
Miss Lilly's Lessons

I went to class today. We were all sitting in what felt like a shallow cave. It was a cave of energy that formed around us, arising from our energy of expectancy and the open mindedness we were all exuding. We were all sitting on benches that formed due to our picturing them there. We did not have to take time to focus and concentrate on creating benches to sit on, we just had a sort of collective expectation that the benches would be there. The bench fit my body well since my energy body is morphing away from my feline shape and beginning to take more of a humanoid shape, with the upright posture and bipedal stance.

Our topic for today's lesson had to do with the basic shape and building blocks of the manifest world. I asked if every soul that took human birth knew this stuff, and the answer was yes—and no. The teacher said we all attend classes and learn this information, but we tend to get so focused on details of our chosen life that we forget. She said that we will be given reminders during our lives on earth. She also said that the information is not static, that we all collectively can, and do, change even the basic patterns for manifestation. She said the main lesson to take from the class is that we are all far more powerful than we remember, and that we all collectively are One.

The teacher told me not to worry about the details of what she was conveying to us; she said to just let the information soak into my consciousness. One of my fellow students expressed grave fear that someone would take over his mind and control him if he was not ever vigilant and attentive to every detail. The teacher then told us that can never happen unless we want it to. She said as long as we attend to our own personal song, we will always be our own self.

The further explanation she gave goes along this line: we each have our own personal chords of vibration that express all that we are, all that we ever have been, and all that we will be according to our current trajectory. This is our personal song. She said we can make soul decisions to change our chords that will then manifest in our lives as beliefs, thoughts, actions, and circumstances. She said that whatever chord another being expresses can be in harmony with ours, or not, and that we gravitate to like-minded songs. She said that the songs or chords of others that clash with ours repel us away from each other, so that we will never be influenced away from our path or song by others.

From what I understand, everything in manifestation is made of waves of vibration. On this side, what you humans call the afterlife, the vibration is of higher octaves compared to the vibratory bandwidth of what humans call being alive. It's a similar concept to the bandwidths of radio waves. The world of the living is made of vibratory expressions of a specific bandwidth, and the world of the other side (where I am) is manifest from a different, yet somewhat over-lapping, bandwidth. There are incalculable other bandwidths of manifestation. For example, you are on one side of our bandwidth and there is another one to the other side. From your perspective our bandwidth is on one side of you and you have another to the other side.

What makes this really complicated to understand is that there are not just two sides to every location of consciousness. There are bandwidths in every direction, from any point of consciousness. The best way I can picture this is to think of a crystal ball—not a smooth one, but one that is faceted. Every side is connected to every other side and every point; every point is connected to every other point and every side. My question here was: If we repel those vibrations that are not harmonious with us, how can every point and facet be connected to every other? I didn't fully understand the answer; from what I understand it has to do with overlapping crystal balls.

This is the explanation of what I learned, as best as I can explain it. The teachers will give better expla-nations when it is your time again to be on this side and attend learning sessions. The way communica-tion happens over here is interesting. We don't speak words, we emanate thought forms that are received and understood. It is all voluntary of course. If someone does not want to receive a thought form, they don't have to. It really is much easier and more efficient.

We also learned about the cosmos and the structure of the Universe. We understand that for each of the heavenly bodies, there is the less dense vibrational version and also the more dense vibrational version. We have been shown that the same pattern manifests at the atomic and subatomic levels as well. I find it fascinating that no matter how large the view, or how tiny the view, the structural pattern is the same. Even more amazing is that the pattern is infinite in both directions.

Chapter Seventeen
Dreamy Coco's Story

I was strolling along a lovely river one day when I received the news that Dreamy Coco had come to this side and was living in a beautiful village not far away. The news came to me with full pictures of the village and the knowledge of the mental path to take to get there. I set my mind to the travel immediately and found myself in the village.

Before my eyes, was Dreamy Coco. I could recognize him by his essence, his song, but he did not look anything like the beautiful feline I had known with his long white hair and his ice blue eyes. Over here, he is a beautiful being of light, somewhat tall and having a male essence. His song sings out from him in magnificent waves of white light, intermingled with sparkling blue light waves.

He saw me and mentally drew me to him in a loving, all-encompassing embrace. His energy and light completely mixed with mine in a way that left me forever changed and uplifted. It was somewhat like being not surrounded by, but more like being completely permeated with love and uplifting wisdom; all of that remains with me to this day.

Dreamy had taken birth as a feline so that he could increase the understanding of his group regarding what beings experience in an earth life. He belongs to a group of guardians that wanted to more fully understand an earth-life experience so they could better assist and guide beings living on earth. Time was an issue when he decided to incarnate because one of the human beings needed assistance and guidance, and needed it very soon. It was a human male who was about to take a very powerful role in governing a large and powerful country but who knew nothing about compassion and love.

This human male was going to need much guidance, and the group wanted to be able to do the best possible job. The body most readily available to Dreamy at the time was a feline who was about to undergo a slow excruciating death from the flea collar that he was rapidly outgrowing. Dreamy had assisted the feline to comfortably slip out of the body and then Dreamy had slipped in. He lived in the body for a while with the pain and fear and then brought himself to My H to be rescued. After the rescue, he had lived out the natural life of the feline body gaining more information for his group and then came back to this side.

His group gained the same experience, information and understanding he was gaining as he lived it, due to their entrained vibrational songs and shared consciousness. He made a deep sacrifice and provided a great service to his group of guardians and to the incarnated beings that they assist. When he arrived back on this side, he was in a more elevated position than when he left, because his song had gained more notes and reached into higher octaves.

Chapter Eighteen
More Learning

From my encounter with Dreamy I came away with a new understanding about manifestation. Everything is an expression of vibratory waves and held together by mathematics, which is really the same thing as music. Music is the same thing as vibration. Mathematics is a way to talk about and describe music. Music is one way we perceive vibration with our sense of hearing.

Another way to say this is that everything has a song. Everything emanates music, if we could only hear it. From another perspective there is an unfathomable expression of an over-arching chord that is the Source for all other chords or notes. As we focus on the manifestation of a certain set of chords and notes (vibratory expressions), we name it a song, or a bird, or a human being, and so on. Listen to all vibratory expressions at the same time and you perceive the Source of it all. We had been given this information in our classes, but now it made more sense. I could see what the teacher/guide had been saying about everything emanating bands of color according to its vibrational output.

I don't know exactly how this principle is used for space travel, but it is. My H and I went on flying saucers many times. She used to work with the extraterrestrials to assist humankind. They would come and get her in the night and she would go assist with their work. There was some work involving the free-will donation of DNA, eggs, and sperm for the re-seeding of future humanity. These "extraterrestrials" were actually human descendants from the future.

Other work involved extraterrestrials who came here from other solar systems and were here as guardians and watchers; they have been on duty here for eons. Their purpose is to do good, such as saving people from harm from other people, protecting earth and her inhabitants from aggressive or violent extraterrestrials, and generally guiding humanity in the direction of respect and love for all.

The technology in the future human spacecraft was amazing. The smaller craft could change the room you were standing in without you moving. If you were in the cockpit area and you wanted to be in the dining area, you just passed your hand over a certain spot on the wall and your surroundings would change. This was not just like a hologram changing; the actual furnishings changed. Where there had been a cockpit chair, now was a table. Where a bank of computers had been on the outside wall, now was a food-cooker and food-producer.

If you wanted to sleep, the same action could bring up the sleeping quarters or shower quarters, or exercise room, and so on. There were other people who remained in the room you left and people who were in the room you went into who had been there before you got there. I would think that the person waving her hand over the spot on the wall was transported from one room to the next, except it was all encapsulated within the same physical space inside the spacecraft. I do not know what this technology is. I just know it is.

These smaller ships came and went between earth and the larger ship. The larger ship was fascinating. More of what I don't understand is that even though human descendants live on earth just as you do, they had to travel a long way in the larger ship to get to us, and it took a long time. The smaller ships were stored in the larger one while they traveled back and forth from their time to ours. The larger ship was a whole city with hundreds of people, including families with children. There were very advanced medical facilities, food growing areas, waste disposal processing areas and so on. On the smaller craft food was produced by a more advanced version of the 3-D and 4-D printers that have just now been developed in our time. These were in use on the larger ship also, but they were growing and producing natural food, too.

My H did not talk about this to many people for the safety of the future humans and for her own peace of mind. She said she did not need the distraction of dealing with people's disbelief or the attention from the groups that would believe her. She had provided some of her DNA and had two twin children that lived with our descendants. We were able to see them when they were very young and then they had to go to the future for a number of years. They did return and we were able to spend time with them again when they were adults.

These types of experiences were very enlightening for me and gave me a whole new perspective on what is. Most humans have such a narrow idea of what life and the world are about. They have such a small idea of what is possible and a limited understanding of what is happening around them. What would the world be like if more humans had a broader view? I'm not sure. I do think they would live a better life if they were not so fearful.

People have such a narrow idea of life and the world, and only a small inkling of what is possible, a limited understanding of what is happening around them.

Chapter Nineteen
About Smelly Beasts
and Charlie Sue Magoo

While living in the city of my birth, Baby Goo came to the end of her earth life and joined all of us on the other side. My H only had two smelly beasts for company then. Now a confession: I have to admit a prejudice. Most of the time humans try to hide their prejudices because they want to be liked, and they think they have to be politically correct or other humans will judge them negatively. Felines just don't care. At least I don't.

What am I talking about? Canines. In my opinion canines are just far lower on the evolutionary scale than felines. It's the way I feel; I just can't help it. I would not want to cause harm to one, but I do want them to stay in their place. They smell. They don't bathe themselves and they grovel. They jump all around and make loud sounds for no apparent reason. They slobber. They just do not seem that intelligent. Are you judging me? Am I not telling the truth? You say that it is wrong to lump all canines into the same category, but show me one, just one, that does not fit this description. My feelings are my feelings.

These feelings lead me to have fudged a little in this recounting of my life. I have referred to the two smelly beasts throughout only in a generic sense, but in fact there were more than two smelly beasts over the decades. They are rather interchangeable, aren't they? They are all so much alike and just reek of begging to be whacked by a feline with claws just slightly stretched out.

When I first entered My H's family there were no smelly beasts. It was just me and Shaba. Then when we moved to the country, My H just had to have "dogs." We first acquired two dogs who were from an unsocialized clan and who had no training at all. They were just not fit for living in a family like ours, so we found them a home on a farm. That should have been enough to dissuade My H from bringing more dogs home; to the contrary, she brought home three.

On the side of the road My H found a cute little all-black puppy that we named Liquorish. A short while later, she found a young hound dog wandering around the side of the road close to where his mom had died after being hit by an automobile. The young dog jumped into the car when she opened the door. She thought the dogs had lived with humans and they had probably been dumped by the side of the road, so she named him Pete; it just seemed to fit with his gangly legs and his gangly personality. Liquorish loved to roll in chicken drop-pings. Pete was just Pete, all legs and gangly. They were both sweet and very canine. They were well-mannered enough as they lived outside in the country, and were very useful I must say for keeping away coyote and patrolling our property.

Next came along a tiny little Pomeranian dog we found on the side of the highway and My H named her Amber for the color of her fur. She was not so well-mannered; we thought that she was definitely dumped by someone who was angry at her for soiling the floor in their house. We let her stay with us anyway.

After sometime, all of these canines went on to the other side for one reason or another. I know, I'm not giving you detail here, but we have already established that canines are just not that interesting. Their intellectual prowess is just about nil.

We were without canines for a few years when My H said it was time to give some more of them a home. We found a beautiful white fur Spitz/Retriever mix at a shelter and brought him home. He was such a smiley, loving beast that we named him, "Happy James." My H believes that for reasons having to do with socializing and mental health there should always be two of a species together, never one alone. So a few days later we went back to the shelter and found a cute little black-and-white Spaniel dog and named her Precious. Happy and Precious were well-mannered and got along well, but they never became best friends. They never soiled inside and went on many walks and car rides and visits to friends. They took trips to Grandma's house and got to sniff around the back yard just like us felines. The canines did other things in the back yard as well!

Eventually Precious's body gave out, so after a few weeks of being sad My H went back to a shelter and found a cute little grey guy, a Lhasa Apso and Poodle mix. He had lived on the streets for most if not all of his life we think. Even though he was a very sweet little guy, she didn't know that when she first met him. She wanted to make sure the new canine would get along with Happy, so she brought Happy into the lobby of the shelter to meet the little grey guy. The two of them walked right up to each other, touched noses, and that was that. Friends forever. My H thinks that when the little guy was living on the streets, he had a large dog as a protector and so he immediately trusted Happy to be his guardian.

A few days after the first meeting with the new little guy, we could go pick him up from the shelter and bring him home. Because My H thought he was Asian, she named him Ling Li. She thought the name meant spiritual prosperity. She found out later that he is actually Tibetan and that Ling is a girl's name. Oops! Too late.

Well, Ling and his brother and sister had been found on the streets running wild and apparently had never had a proper home or a human to care for them. Ling was afraid of My H for several days and would not go near her. I guess humans had treated him badly on the streets and then when he was rescued, he got bathed repeatedly due to his stench, and then they neutered him. He was a year-and-a-half-old then and did not take kindly to those actions. They also shaved all of his hair off because the stink would not wash out of it.

It was very apparent that Ling thought Happy had rescued him from the shelter and he adored Happy. He would just watch him and stare at him for hours with love-eyes. Ling copied everything Happy did. Finally, he noticed that Happy was not afraid of My H and even took food from her hand. He also noticed that he and Happy did not have to beg for food or live on the streets with its dangers and discomforts. Ling finally began to trust My H and became socialized. At that point he became a "skin dog" and did not want to leave My H's side. He always felt the need to touch her or to be able to see where she was. He cried if she left for work or went to the grocery store, so she tried to take Happy and Ling with her to as many places as she could.

Happy lived to be about 18 years old. Finally, when he knew his little buddy was safe and well loved, he left his earth life. Ling had been in the family about two years then and he was so lonely that My H knew he needed a new canine family member soon. My H's friend found two small girl canines lost on the street. The poor little things were skinny and hungry. They had been dumped at a vet's office a week before, but the people working there did not take them in or feed them. My H brought one home and we named her Joy Light. Funny thing is Joy had formal obedience training. We wondered if she had been used as a show dog and was dumped for not performing as well as her owner had wished. Who knows?

Chapter Twenty
Love Returns

My H always said that love always returns to love. She said that humans who love each other will be together on the other side as often as they wish to and that if they incarnate on earth again, they will gravitate together or plan a life together. She says that her pets will always return to her. (I resent being referred to as a pet as if I were a lesser being, or as if I were owned!) She said that when a pet returns to her, she feels soul recognition but is not always certain who the pet was in a previous life. It is only when she realized that she was not able to remember much about the life and death of a certain pet that she realized that they must have re-incarnated into the family again.

When I heard her talking about this one day, she said that even though she felt a very intense love for Charlie Sue Magoo, she is unable to remember Charlie Sue as a kitten or how or when she came into the family or how she died. She could remember her beautiful shining grey fur and kissing her on the top of her head. She knew that Charlie was the last of the felines to go and she remembered that she could not see very well and that was how she came up with her name. My H said that we do this type of forgetting on purpose so we can have new experiences that are not tainted by the past. She said that Charlie Sue Magoo had returned to the family as Joy Light, the little blind dog. She said that the soul that was here as a feline, Charlie Sue, was the same soul that came back as the canine, Joy Light.

My H said she felt soul recognition the first time she saw Joy Light, felt love immediately and knew she wanted to take her home with her. Sometime later she realized that Joy was Charlie Sue and had returned as a small dog. She said that Charlie/Joy's soul was learning lessons by having very poor eyesight and was also providing an example for her, My H, at the same time. She said that Charlie/Joy taught her about independence when possible, reliance on others when needed, trust, self-assertiveness, fearlessness, adaptiveness, flexibility, and love. I think Charlie/Joy taught us that who we are, where we are in life, and our life choices are not accidental; that we are each looked after, guided, protected, and loved.

For me, this shows that I chose my last life, am in the process of choosing my next life, and that I am responsible for the choices I make, the results of those choices and choosing differently if I don't like the results. The responsibility for my experiences is mine.

Chapter Twenty One
Born Again

My H spoke of her past lives on more than one occasion. I want to share these here so that humans can begin to understand that life is etermal. I have used My H's words to express these lifetimes and put her past-life memories in the order that seems logical to me; but in truth, I do not know the exact order and for the ones that were not on Earth, I do not know where they were. So in the very first one I will recount, she and the other beings in her life wave were each in the form of a vortex of colorful energy that had varying amounts of movement and color-change depending on feelings and thoughts. They took the shape of a cyclone with the broad part in the upward position and the tail pointed downward. In this life-wave, there were no bipeds or animal shapes or any "meat bodies" at all. Similar to humans, the younger the being, the smaller the vortex or body of energy and light. They had family groups and couples and communities. They had feelings of love, devotion, and compassion. My H remembered being a young child in the family and remembered her mother and an older sister. She does not remember any male energies in that life wave. The process for birth was a separating off of energy from her mother.

The separated energy became a separate entity who initially had the energy manifested by the mother at birth. The offspring would then gradually develop her own energy field, wisdom, feelings, and thoughts as she grew larger, stronger, and more mature. Everyone grew into individual expressions of the Oneness. There was a feeling of closeness and love, with communication being by emanating waves of energy. When recounting this lifetime, My H spoke of a suffocating feeling, like the space between beings was heavy with vibratory waves.

◎◎◎

She spoke of being a fairy like being in one life and was a member of the privileged class. She would flit around all day enjoying herself among what she believes were flowers and plants. In this life she pursued pleasure without much care for the well being of others. It was a peaceful, happy life of enjoyment for her that she lived on a feeling basis. She said it was almost the complete opposite of her most current life as a human, which was dominated by thoughts with feelings a distant second.

◎◎◎

There was one life where she was a scientist caught up in the middle of a war that she did not even know had started. It was not on Earth and in many ways the civilization was far more advanced than current

Earth civilizations. She was alone on an outpost on a small body in space similar to a miniature planet. She thought it might have been an artificial construct that was placed in space for the sole purpose of scientific experimentation.

There was a science station with a lab and she collected samples and conducted experiments. Her transportation back to home was way overdue and her situation was getting desperate since food, water, and fuel were in very short supply. Suddenly one day an enemy ship appeared in the sky and attacked her. She said these beings looked like fore-bearers of a particular type of people that are living on Earth today. The being who was supposed to come for her and take her home had been killed in the war. She said this being was her life partner in this most recent earth life.

◎◎◎

Another life was on Earth when hominids were very rudimentary. Language was grunts and growls. They did use signals such as carved emblems on trees or beating specific rhythms on logs. My H remembered herself as a male, standing barefoot at the edge of a grassy plane looking out over the top of the grass. Her impression was that she was not very tall, maybe three-to-three-and-a-half-feet in height. She said she was wearing a type of body covering made of a brown fur pelt. It had an opening that went over the head and draped over her left shoulder with a hole for the left arm. Her right shoulder was bare and the garment was open most of the way down her right side to her waist. Holes had been deliberately cut in the skin for her head and arms and it hung close to her body all the way to her hip area. It was the customary body-covering for the clan and was designed for utilitarian and protective purposes.

She could look down and see her body as thick, muscular, and covered in sparse brown hair about two inches long. She said her feet and toes were shorter and wider than current human toes and feet. She was alone there and she thinks she was hunting. The feeling she had in the scene was one of peaceful alertness with intention. She said she could feel her brain as alert and active, but concrete. She did not have a philosophical bent; no self-questioning or self-doubt. She said she lacked the type of neurotic self-awareness humans tend to have today.

◎◎◎

There was a life as a young male in early Greco-Roman times. She was born with an inability to speak, and physical deformities in her body and face. There had been discussions at birth whether to kill her or let her live. They let her live, but ignored and neglected her. Although mute and ugly, she was very intelligent and understood everything. That made it hurt even more that no one spoke to her, showed her affection or love, or tried to teach her anything. She felt very lonely, hurt, and unloved. She was never allowed out in public, as the family was ashamed of her and did not want anyone outside of the family and trusted servants to see her or even know she existed. Her father in that lifetime was her mother in this most recent lifetime.

At about age seven, she was feeling angry and wanting attention, so she went running around in a room where she knew she should not be. It was like a display room in a museum with vases and statues on pedestals. She bumped into one, knocking it down and shattering it. From then on, she was banished to the back yard with the dogs. She was very sorry for what she had done and thought if given a chance she would never break anything again. From then on she was even more neglected.

When food was thrown out into the yard for the dogs she had to fight to grab some without getting bitten. As she grew, she began to be able to climb over the wall and wander around on the property. When the family discovered this she was chained by the neck to the wall at the very back left side of the yard. The yard was covered with fruit and nut trees and she was able to reach enough to eat. Servants would water the trees and put water in a bowl that sat near her. As she grew, the chain around her neck became tighter and tighter. Maybe someone would have noticed and made a larger collar or set her free, but she did not live long enough to find out.

Her mother in that life wanted nothing to do with her and felt that she was to blame for the deformed, defective child. It was the father that saw to it that she was provided with food and water and allowed to live. At one point her father had to travel to a distant city to haggle over and to pay taxes. This was a several-month process. During this time for some reason, her mother decided to take the servants, household goods, and dogs, and move. She was left chained to the back wall. There was no one to put water in her bowl and with no one to water the trees, they dried up and died. The cats that had made the yard their home began to leave and she assisted the small, young cats over the wall. She was left alone to starve, feeling unloved, and unlovable; she died of thirst.

Long before Europeans began arriving in what is now called North America, she lived as an indigenous man living in the now southwest United States. Her role at that time was one of contemplation and spiritual pursuits. She remembers being in tall rock formations in bright sunlight where she would sit in a see-through opening in a rock that had an arch overhead. Here she would sit and meditate for days, sometimes even weeks. She would attune to the Great Spirit and the Wisdom of the Ages. This is where she died alone and in tune. She had a sense of having done something wrong and having been banished from her tribe.

◎◎◎

She remembered that during World War II, she was a Jewish female living in Germany. Her family was forced to move into the ghetto, and they moved the family business into a small shop with two glass display-windows at the front of the store that were separated by the front door. Her father was a successful printer and book-seller. In the ghetto, he would display books and other items in the two front windows. During one of the raids conducted by the thugs, she saw the store windows being broken; the shop being ransacked, and her father being killed. She could not help and had to run away into hiding. She worked with the underground resistance from that point on and even took a fairly high-ranking German soldier as a boyfriend in order to obtain information. She was able to do this because she could "pass." She had shoulder-length wavy honey-blond hair and green eyes. Eventually she was betrayed and her boyfriend provided her with death by firing squad rather than sending her to a concentration camp.

When My H began to remember her past lives, she thought that her lifetimes of suffering and pain were self-inflicted and caused by her own consciousness and underlying beliefs. She believed she was punishing herself for a past life where her clan was in conflict with another. When she and the other males of her clan were away hunting, the females and children of her clan were tortured and killed. She and the other males of her clan were so enraged that they raided the opposing clan's camp and tortured and killed everyone.

Because she was actually a very loving and empathetic soul, she carried tremendous guilt over her actions for the rest of that life. After she died, her guilt kept her from enjoying the other side or partaking of all of its advantages. She was so dark in her thoughts and feelings that she gravitated to outer darkness. Her consciousness was in suspension in a dark corner of space for eons. In fact it was so long that she had forgotten that it was her own state of consciousness that had caused her to be there.

For a very long time, she thought she had been banished to outer darkness by others who had judged her. When she finally began to remember that it was her own feelings of guilt and self-condemnation that caused her to be in her outer darkness prison, she was able to escape the prison and renew her cycle of incarnating into form. Even then her guilt was not over and she began to create lifetimes for herself where she was alone, or mistreated, or both.

Even in her most recent lifetime, the one where I was with her as Miss Lily, she caused herself much torture, pain, and rejection by others. She finally realized what she was doing and began to heal her consciousness. Before she left this earth life, she had forgiven herself and removed her consciousness from the wheel of births and deaths. She understood the concepts of grace and forgiveness as well as self-love and self-acceptance. She also understood that we each create our own reality and once we accept that power to create we can change whatever we want about ourselves and our lives.

From my point of view I think all human suffering is a reflection of how people feel about themselves. If we feel unworthy of love, wealth, success, good health, and happiness, we will make certain that we don't allow ourselves these joys of life. How many humans have I seen that sabotage themselves time after time, all of them with their own individual theme. One has a constant shortage of money; another feels that she does not have friends and no one likes her. Yet another experiences one unhappy or abusive relationship after another yet never learns to choose differently. I must say, I have seen some work on themselves through counseling or psychotherapy and make changes to some degree in some areas of their lives. I have seen others who undergo a spiritual awakening of various sorts and make sweeping changes to all or nearly all aspects of their lives and choices.

As a whole, humans seem to be on the rise in their conscious awareness. It does seem to me that there are those who lag behind because of not wanting to let go of a sense of power and superiority. In our lessons over here, we have learned that part of the current human life wave will move on into the more loving existence and rarified ethers of the Aquarian Age and some will remain with the more war-like, denser ethers of the Piscean Age. I wonder what do you think and which existence will you choose for yourself?